D1391384

New contact details:
School Libraries
Resources Service
Phone 020 8359 3931
Fax 020 8201 3018
slrs@barnet.gov.uk

withdrawn

30131 04122085 3

LONDON BOROUGH OF BARNET

Happy Ever After

For Jenny
S.W.

LONDON BOROUGH OF BARNET SCHOOL LIBRARIES RESOURCES SERVICE	
19-Dec-05	PETERS
JF	£8.99

ORCHARD BOOKS
338 Euston Road, London NW1 3BH
Orchard Books Australia
Hachette Children's Books
Level 17/207, Kent Street, Sydney, NSW 2000
ISBN 1 84362 526 1 (hardback)
ISBN 1 84362 534 2 (paperback)
First published in Great Britain in 2005
First paperback publication in 2006
Text © Tony Bradman 2005 Illustrations © Sarah Warburton 2005
The rights of Tony Bradman to be identified as the author
and of Sarah Warburton to be identified as the illustrator of this
work have been asserted by them in accordance with the Copyright,
Designs and Patents Act, 1988. A CIP catalogue record for this book is
available from the British Library.
1 3 5 7 9 10 8 6 4 2 (hardback)
1 3 5 7 9 10 8 6 4 2 (paperback)
The text paper this book is printed on is certified by the Forest
Stewardship Council (FSC). FSC products with percentage claims
meet environmental requirements to be ancient-forest friendly.
The printer Cox & Wyman holds FSC chain of custody TT-COC-2063.
Printed in Great Britain by Cox & Wyman, CPI Group.

Tony Bradman

Happy Ever After

CINDERELLA
AND THE MEAN QUEEN

Illustrated by Sarah Warburton

ORCHARD BOOKS

"Do get a move on, Cinderella," said her husband, Prince Charming. "You know Mother hates it when we're late for dinner."

"Just coming, sweetheart," Cinderella
murmured, checking herself one last
time in her full-length mirror.

"What do you think of this dress and these boots?" she said. "I'm trying out a whole new style."

"Er...they're fine," the prince said quickly. "Can we go now?"

Cinderella sighed, and they set off. She loved the prince, and he loved her, and she'd thought her troubles were over when they'd got married. But it was hard living with Prince Charming's parents in the castle.

Everything was so posh and luxurious, and she missed the little cottage where she had lived with her father.

Sometimes she even missed her Wicked Stepmother and the Ugly Sisters. They didn't seem too bad when she thought about them now.

At least, not compared to Prince Charming's mother, the queen...

"And WHERE have you two been?" the queen roared as the prince and Cinderella entered the royal dining room. "Your soup is getting cold!"

"Sorry, Mother," said the prince, as they sat in their usual places.

"You look lovely this evening, my dear," said the king, the prince's father, smiling at Cinderella. He was always very sweet to her.

"Hah! You never pay me compliments like that," snapped the queen. The king opened his mouth to speak, but the queen held up her spoon and glared.

"Don't bother. I know I look dreadful these days," the queen went on. "But I can't spend all day prettifying myself. I have more important things to do!"

Cinderella had a feeling the queen would quite like the king to pay her compliments. She had sometimes seen the queen glancing at herself in mirrors and sighing deeply when she thought no one else was around...

The queen was particularly horrible to Cinderella that evening. Later, Cinderella sat at her dressing table and sobbed. The prince put his arm round her.

"Don't take it to heart, Cinders," he said softly, passing her a royal hanky. "I'm certain Mother likes you. Er...deep down, anyway."

"No she doesn't," Cinderella wailed,
and blew her nose.

"She hates me. I've heard her saying
I'm useless, and how I'm only here
because of the Fairy Godmother. Well,
I've had enough. I'll prove to her that
I'm not just a pretty face."

"Really?" said the prince. "What do you have in mind?"

"I'm going to get a job," said Cinderella. "A good one, too."

"Gosh!" said the prince, his eyes wide. "I'm impressed already!"

In the morning, Cinderella scanned the "Jobs Vacant" pages of the *Forest Times,* and she soon found something. Fairy Tale Fashions, the smartest clothes store in the forest, was looking for a sales executive.

Cinderella had been interested in clothes and fashion ever since her own transformation. She often looked at other people and thought she might be able to give them some good advice on how to make more of themselves...

So she phoned for an application
form, quickly filled it in, sent it back,
and waited nervously. Her phone rang
the next day.

"Oh hi, yes, this is Cinderella Charming," she said. "I've got the job? Wow, fantastic! But wait, aren't you going to interview me or anything? You're not, I see...When do I start? Nine o'clock tomorrow? Er...OK."

Cinderella was surprised it had been so easy. Surely it should have been a bit harder - after all, she'd never had a proper job before. Then she shrugged, and started choosing an outfit to wear.

The prince insisted on taking her to work in the royal coach. But when they arrived, things weren't quite as Cinderella was expecting...

The royal guards had to hold back a large crowd, and wild cheering broke out as Cinderella walked up the red carpet that led to the store's entrance.

The manager and staff of Fairy Tale
Fashions were there to greet her.

"I don't understand," said Cinderella.
"What are all these people doing here?
I didn't think your sale started for
another couple of months yet."

"They're here to see you, Your
Highness," said the manager, curtseying.
"I mean, what a story! Rags to riches,
a grand ball, midnight, the glass
slipper - it's all so romantic! Now, there's
a TV news crew waiting..."

Poor Cinderella's heart sank. She realised Fairy Tale Fashions didn't have a real job for her. They just wanted to use her for publicity. So she let the TV crew film her, and signed autographs.

But then she got in the royal coach
and went home. She ran up to her room
and burst into tears.

After dinner that evening, the royal family watched the news on the royal television set, and the queen was even more horrible than before.

"Complete waste of time..." Cinderella heard her say. "She'll be useless...never amount to anything...she's not even that pretty..."

Cinderella didn't go back to Fairy Tale Fashions. She phoned them the next morning and said she didn't want the job.

Then she went for a long walk in the royal gardens, and wondered what to do. Perhaps she could apply for another job? But the same thing would probably happen again. After all, everybody knew her name and her story.

Cinderella was so fed up she thought for a moment of trying to get in touch with the Fairy Godmother. But she realised that would only prove the queen was right about her.

No, whatever she did, she would have to do it without any help... And then Cinderella had an utterly brilliant idea.

She spent the rest of that week
thinking and planning and surfing the
Forest Web on the royal computer to see
if she had any competition. But nobody
else seemed to be doing what she had
in mind...

And so a month later she launched her business, Cinderella Makeovers Unlimited, with a big party in the royal ballroom. Lots of people were invited, and the event was covered by Forest TV and all the newspapers.

"Huh, they're only interested because she's one of us," the queen said snootily. But Cinderella didn't have time to worry. She was too busy showing everyone what she could do.

A couple of people at the party had volunteered to be transformed, and the results were pretty amazing.

"Wow!" said Little Red Riding Hood's granny when she saw herself.

"I love the way you've done my hair...and these clothes are fantastic! I look at least twenty years younger. I can't thank you enough!"

The queen didn't say a word. She did
seem impressed, though.

Soon Cinderella had lots of clients. She worked her magic on every witch in the forest, several trolls, the Bad Fairy, and dozens of wicked stepmothers, including her own, who turned up one day with the Ugly Sisters...

"If I can sort those three out, I can do anything!" thought Cinderella.

It was a real triumph, and led to her getting her own series on Forest TV, The Cinders Show.

And the Wicked Stepmother and the
Ugly Sisters were so grateful they
begged Cinderella to forgive them for
being horrible to her in the past.
Cinderella did, of course, and from that
day on they were great friends.

And not long after that, somebody else came to see Cinderella in her salon. It was the queen. She came in, sat down, and smiled nervously.

"I know I haven't been the best of mothers-in-law to you, Cinderella," she said. "But I've seen your show on television, and I just wondered..."

Cinderella smiled too, and got straight to work. She tackled the queen's hair...and make-up...and clothes...and this time she surpassed even herself.

That evening, Cinderella and the
queen walked into the royal dining
room together. The prince and the king
sat with their mouths open.

"My goodness!" said the king at last,
staring at his wife, his eyes misty with
admiration and love. "You look, well...
absolutely stunning, dear!"

The queen was delighted, and so was
Prince Charming.

"Well done, Cinders!" he said, and
kissed her...

And so Cinderella and Prince Charming and his parents and everyone else in the forest who needed brilliant fashion and beauty advice lived...

HAPPILY EVER AFTER!

Happy Ever After

Written by Tony Bradman
Illustrated by Sarah Warburton

These books are available from all good bookshops, or can be ordered direct
from the publisher: Orchard Books, PO BOX 29, Douglas IM99 1BQ.
Credit card orders please telephone 01624 836000 or fax 01624 837033 or
visit our Internet site: www.wattspub.co.uk or
e-mail: bookshop@enterprise.net for details.

To order please quote title, author and ISBN and your full name and
address. Cheques and postal orders should be made payable to 'Bookpost
plc.' Postage and packing is FREE within the UK
(overseas customers should add £1.00 per book).

Prices and availability are subject to change.